SYLVIA LONG'S

BIG BOOK

for Small Children

To my mother, Marion Lyman Carlisle,
a tough act to follow.

Library of Congress Cataloging-in-Publication Data available.

ISBN 978-0-8118-3441-4

Manufactured in China.

MIX
Paper from
responsible sources
FSC™ C104723

Design by Sara Gillingham Studio.
Typeset in Ernestine, Naive, and Primer Print.
The illustrations in this book were rendered in watercolor.

"Who has seen the wind?" excerpt by Christina Rossetti
"I've got a pretty tulip" from "Little Phillis" excerpt by Kate Greenaway
"My Shadow" excerpt by Robert Louis Stevenson, adapted by Sylvia Long
"Golden Slumbers" excerpt by Thomas Dekker

10 9 8 7 6 5 4 3 2 1

Chronicle Books LLC
680 Second Street
San Francisco, California 94107

Chronicle Books—we see things differently.
Become part of our community at www.chroniclekids.com.

SYLVIA LONG'S
BIG BOOK
for Small Children

Collected and illustrated
by Sylvia Long

chronicle books · san francisco

A NOTE FROM THE ARTIST

Many years ago I had the pleasure of illustrating a collection of Mother Goose rhymes. It has been exciting to see so many people embrace that book, but it was an enormous undertaking, and, really, I never thought I would illustrate such a "big" book again. But as the years passed, my sons grew up and I became a grandmother. It wasn't long before I began to remember rhymes and stories that were an important part of my childhood, as well as lullabies, sung to me by my mother or played by my father on his recorder, that I wanted to pass down to a new generation.

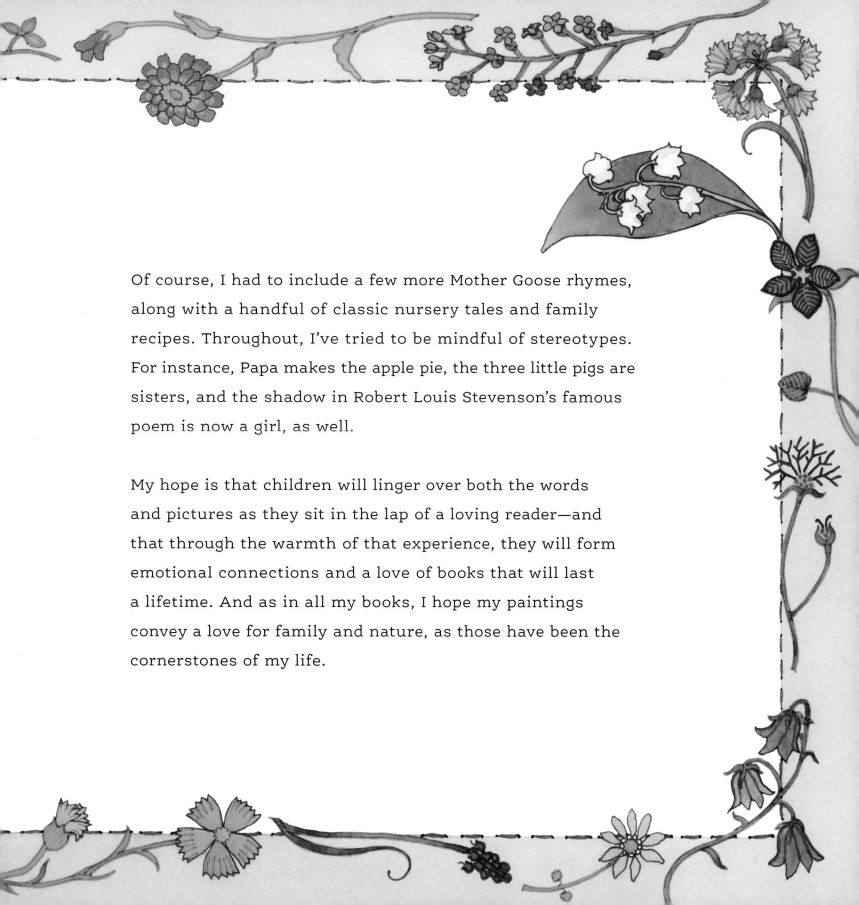

Of course, I had to include a few more Mother Goose rhymes, along with a handful of classic nursery tales and family recipes. Throughout, I've tried to be mindful of stereotypes. For instance, Papa makes the apple pie, the three little pigs are sisters, and the shadow in Robert Louis Stevenson's famous poem is now a girl, as well.

My hope is that children will linger over both the words and pictures as they sit in the lap of a loving reader—and that through the warmth of that experience, they will form emotional connections and a love of books that will last a lifetime. And as in all my books, I hope my paintings convey a love for family and nature, as those have been the cornerstones of my life.

GOOD MORNING,

merry sunshine,
How did you wake so soon?
You frightened all the stars away
And shined away the moon.

Come, my dear children,
Up is the sun.
Birds are all singing,
And morn has begun.

socks

MY CLOTHES

pajamas

slippers

nightgown

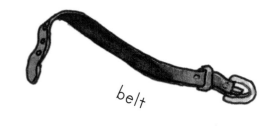

belt

dress

pants

sweater

blouse

T-shirt

overalls

leggings

sandals

Mary Janes

shorts

shoes

skirt

FAMILIES

Families can be big or small,
near or far,
But all families
are filled with love.

MY BOOKS AND TOYS

I had a little hobbyhorse,
And it was dapple gray.
Its head was made of pea-straw,
Its tail was made of hay.

Smiling girls and rosy boys
Come and buy my little toys.
Monkeys made of gingerbread
And sugar horses painted red.

rubber spatula

IN THE KITCHEN

mixing bowl

wooden spoon

whisk

measuring cups

dish towel

sponge

tablespoon

teaspoon

griddle

hot pad

skillet

saucepan

cookie sheet

metal spatula

Great A, little a,
This is pancake day!
Toss the ball high,
Throw the ball low.
Those that come after
May sing hi-ho!

GRANDMA'S CORNMEAL PANCAKES

SERVES 6

In a medium bowl, sift:
- 1 cup (140 grams) flour
- ¾ cup (105 grams) cornmeal
- 2 tablespoons sugar
- 1 teaspoon baking powder
- 1 teaspoon salt

Gently stir together to combine. Set aside.

In a large bowl, put:
- 2 cups (480 millilitres) buttermilk
- 2 eggs, slightly beaten
- 2 tablespoons vegetable oil
- 1 teaspoon baking soda

Stir together to combine.

Add the flour mixture to the buttermilk mixture and stir gently until combined.

For each pancake, pour ¼ cup (60 millilitres) batter onto a hot, lightly oiled griddle. When golden brown on the bottom, flip once to brown the other side.

Serve hot with sliced fresh peaches, plain Greek yogurt, and some brown sugar or maple syrup.

MY OUTDOOR CLOTHES

winter coat

sun hat

scarf

snow boots

winter hat

gloves

earmuffs

snowsuit

mittens

rain hat

swimsuit

raincoat

swimming trunks

rain boots

Who has seen the wind?
Neither I nor you.
But when the leaves hang trembling,
The wind is passing through.

Here we go round the mulberry bush,
The mulberry bush, the mulberry bush.
Here we go round the mulberry bush,
On a cold and frosty morning.

The soft, balmy breezes are blowing.
The roses and poppies are gay.
The farmer is busily mowing,
While birds and butterflies play.

One misty, moisty morning
When cloudy was the weather,
I chanced to meet an old man
  clothed all in leather.
He began to compliment,
  and I began to grin,
"How do you do,
  and how do you do?
And how do you do, again?"

Dr. Foster went to Glo'ster
In a shower of rain.
She stepped in a puddle,
Right up to her middle,
And never went there again.

THE THREE LITTLE PIGS

ONCE UPON A TIME,

there were three little pigs who set out to make their own way in the world.

The first little pig spied a tall strawstack. By hollowing out the center, she made a house.

"That was easy," she said.

The second little pig collected sticks and branches, which she stacked to make a small shelter.

"That was easy," she said.

The third little pig walked and walked until she found a hilltop clearing. She worked for days, making bricks of straw and mud, and then she stacked them to make the walls of her small house straight and strong.

One chilly day, the first little pig heard a wolf growling outside her straw house.

"Let me in! Let me in!" growled the wolf.

"Not by the hair on my chinny-chin-chin!" squealed the first little pig.

"Then I'll huff, and I'll puff, and I'll blow your house in!" answered the wolf.

And he huffed, and he puffed, and with one strong blow, he split the house into a hundred pieces that drifted across the wheat field.

The first little pig ran like the wind and did not look back until she was safely inside the second little pig's stick house in the forest.

Before long, the two little pigs heard the wolf pacing outside.

"Let me in! Let me in!" snarled the wolf.

"Not by the hair on our chinny-chin-chins!" the two little pigs squealed.

"Then I'll huff and I'll puff, and I'll blow your house in!" answered the wolf.

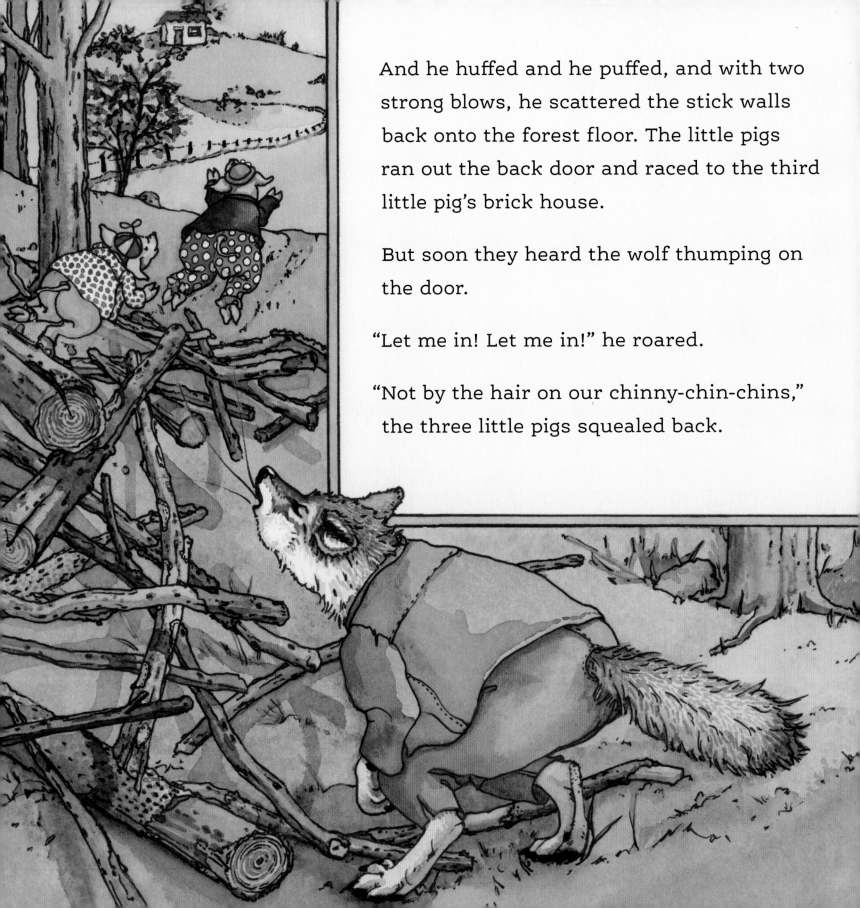

And he huffed and he puffed, and with two strong blows, he scattered the stick walls back onto the forest floor. The little pigs ran out the back door and raced to the third little pig's brick house.

But soon they heard the wolf thumping on the door.

"Let me in! Let me in!" he roared.

"Not by the hair on our chinny-chin-chins," the three little pigs squealed back.

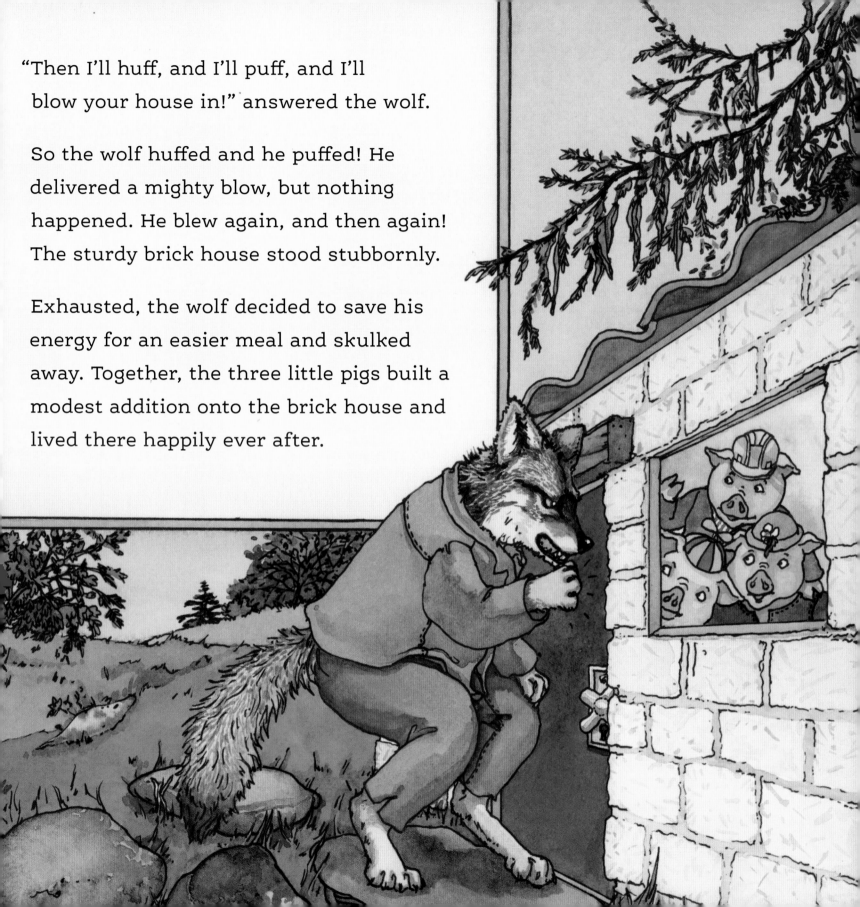

"Then I'll huff, and I'll puff, and I'll blow your house in!" answered the wolf.

So the wolf huffed and he puffed! He delivered a mighty blow, but nothing happened. He blew again, and then again! The sturdy brick house stood stubbornly.

Exhausted, the wolf decided to save his energy for an easier meal and skulked away. Together, the three little pigs built a modest addition onto the brick house and lived there happily ever after.

THE END

Little Tommy Tucker
Sings for his supper.
What shall we give him?
Brown bread and butter.

play a game

plant a seed

smell a flower

MY GARDEN

Take care of your garden
And keep it from weeds.
Fill it with sunshine,
Kind words, and kind deeds.

tomatoes

lettuce

kale

sweet peas

beans

carrots

radishes

Swiss chard

grapes

strawberries

"Cantaloupes! Cantaloupes!"
"What is the price?"
"Eight for a dollar,
 And all very nice."

pineapples

bleeding heart

poppy

daffodil

baby blue eyes

heather

FLOWERS

tiger lily

bluebell

rose

zinnia

petunia

morning glory

tulip

lily of the valley

lady's slipper

nasturtium

snowdrop

I've got a pretty tulip
In my little flower bed.
If you would like, I'll give it you—
It's yellow, striped with red.

shy

SOMETIMES
I FEEL

sad

happy

proud

MY SHADOW

I have a little shadow
    that goes in and out with me,
And what can be the use of her
    is more than I can see.
She is very, very like me
    from the heels up to the head;
And I see her jump before me,
    when I jump into my bed.

AT SCHOOL

Very little ones are we,
But we've learned our ABCs.
We can read and we can spell,
And we obey our teacher well.

Hickory dickory, sackory down
Which is the way to Richmond town?
Turn to the left, then turn to the right,
And you may get there by Saturday night.

THE
LITTLE
RED HEN

The Little Red 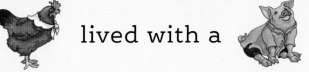 lived with a , a ,

and a on a wee farm. One day, the Little

Red was thinking about how much she liked

corn bread. She went to the market and bought

some corn seeds.

   "Who will help plant this corn?" the Little Red

 asked her friends. "Not I," said the .

"Not I," said the . "Not I," said the .

So the Little Red planted the corn by herself.

   All summer, the Little Red worked in the

garden, watering and pulling weeds until the corn

stalks were tall and the ears of corn were ripe.

"Who will help pick the corn?" she asked.

"Not I," said the . "Not I," said the .

"Not I," said the . So the Little Red

harvested the corn by herself, dried the kernels,

and ground them into cornmeal.

"Who will help make corn bread?" she asked.

"Not I," said the . "Not I," said the .

"Not I," said the . So the Little Red

made the corn bread by herself. As it baked, the

sweet aroma drifted through an open window.

The Little Red called out, "Who plans to

eat this corn bread?" "I will!" said the .

"I will!" said the . "I will!" said the .

"No you won't," said the Little Red .

"I bought the corn seed, planted it, watered and

weeded it, dried the kernels, ground them into meal,

and made the corn bread by myself. Now I will eat it,

by myself." And she did, right to the very last crumb.

THE LITTLE RED HEN'S CORN BREAD

SERVES 9

Preheat the oven to 400°F (200°C).

Butter an 8-by-8-inch (20-by-20-centimetre) baking pan.

In a medium bowl, put:

- 1¼ cups (175 grams) flour
- ¾ cup (105 grams) cornmeal
- 4 tablespoons (50 grams) sugar
- 3 teaspoons baking powder
- ½ teaspoon salt

Stir to combine. Add:

- 1 cup (240 millilitres) milk
- 1 egg, well beaten
- 3 tablespoons butter, melted

Stir to mix well. Pour the batter into the prepared baking pan.

Bake for 30 minutes, or until golden brown.

OPPOSITES

over   inside   push

under   outside   pull

wet

high

open

dry

low

shut

One, two, three, four, five,
Once I caught a fish alive.
Six, seven, eight, nine, ten,
But I let it go again.

6 7 8 9 10

Why did you let it go?
Because it bit my finger so!
Which finger did it bite?
The little one upon the right.

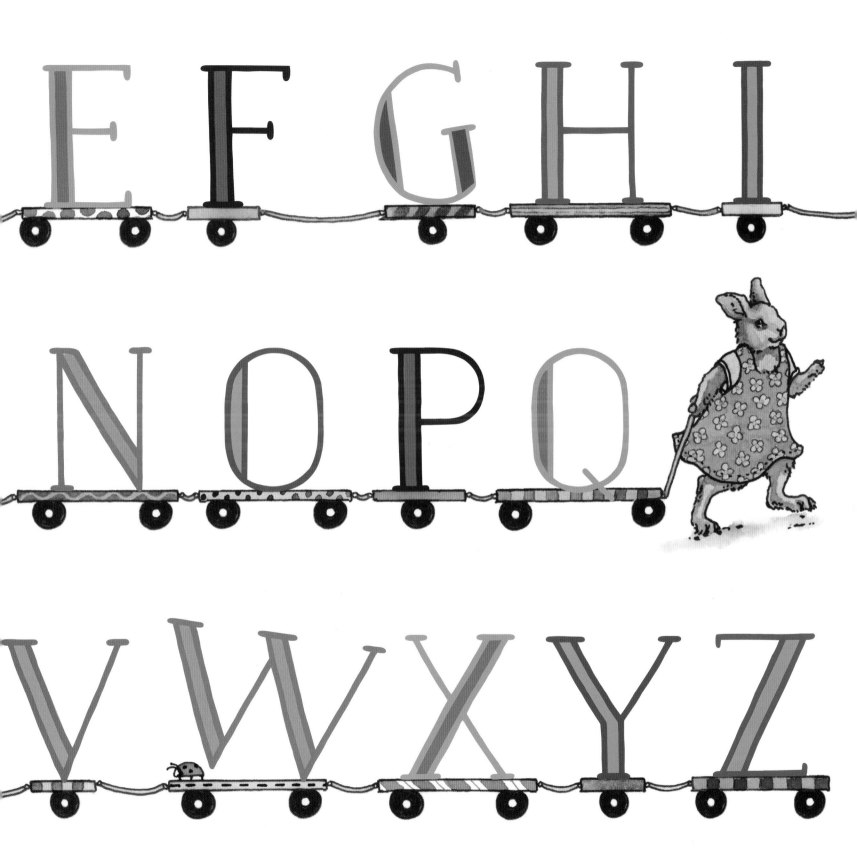

green

blue

yellow

orange

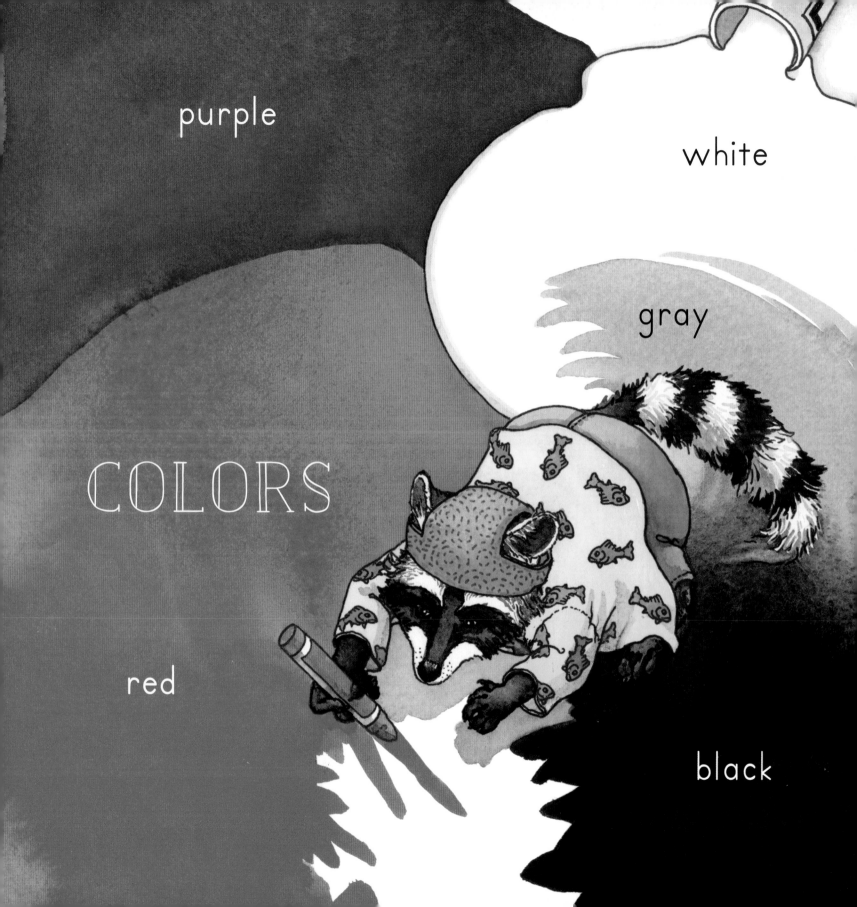

purple

white

gray

COLORS

red

black

I CAN

swim

play hide-and-seek

pull a wagon

take a walk

find a rock

climb a tree

GOING PLACES

car

school bus

ambulance

pickup truck

eighteen-wheeler

tricycle

bicycle

wagon

fishing boat

sailboat

canoe

airplane

helicopter

space shuttle

tractor

fire engine

train

cruise ship

rowboat

I can look . . . but not touch.

At the
BEACH

Can you find shapes
in this picture?

circle

square

heart

diamond

oval

triangle

rectangle

star

At the PARK

triangle

cymbal

tambourin

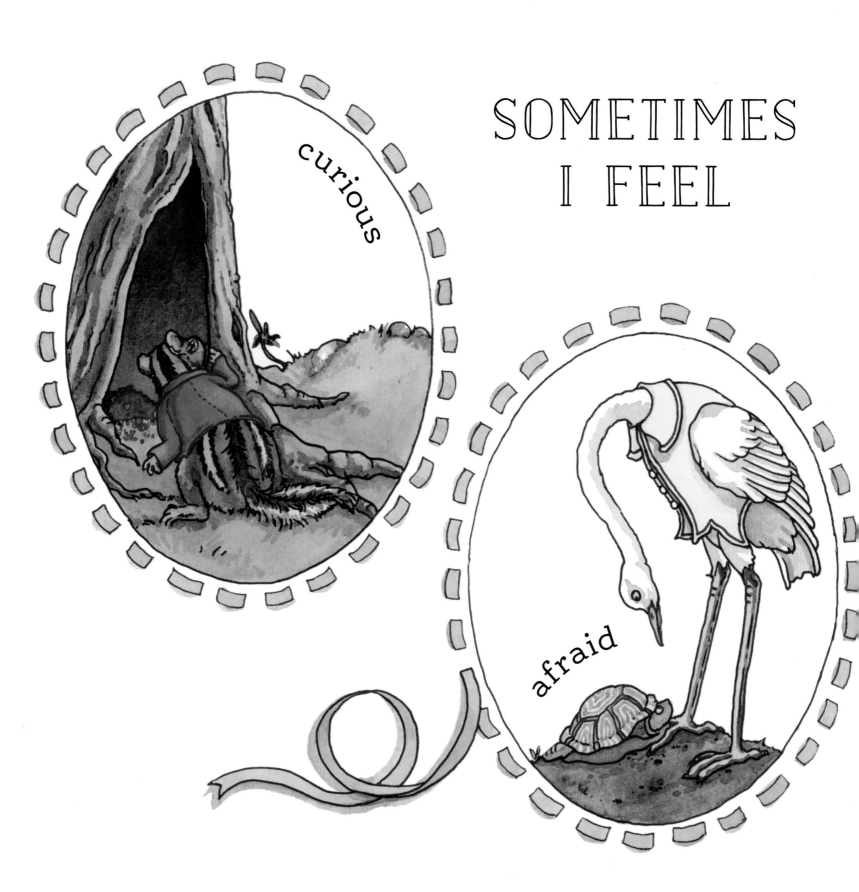

curious

SOMETIMES
I FEEL

afraid

frustrated

surprised

An apple pie, when it looks nice,
Would make one long to have a slice.
But if the taste should prove so, too,
I fear one slice would scarcely do.
So to prevent my asking twice,
Please, Papa, cut a good large slice.

GOLDILOCKS AND THE THREE BEARS

IN THE FOREST

lived a family of three bears.

There was great big Papa Bear, middle-size Mama Bear, and small Baby Bear. One morning, they went for a walk while their porridge cooled.

That same morning, in another part of the forest, curious little Goldilocks also went for a walk.

When Goldilocks spied a house, she gently pushed the door. It opened, and Goldilocks went inside.

Inside was a table with three chairs: a great big chair, a middle-size chair, and a small chair. On the table were three bowls of porridge: a big one, a middle-size one, and a small one. Goldilocks was hungry.

She sat on the great big chair and tried the big bowl of porridge. The chair was too hard and the porridge was too hot.

She sat on the middle-size chair and tried the middle-size bowl of porridge. The chair was too soft and the porridge was too cold.

When Goldilocks sat on the small chair and tried the small bowl of porridge, it was just right and she ate every bit. When she hopped off the small chair, it tipped over and broke into pieces.

Goldilocks went upstairs, where she found three beds: a great big bed, a middle-size bed, and a small bed. Goldilocks was tired.

She sat on the big bed. It was too hard.

She sat on the middle-size bed. It was too soft.

When Goldilocks lay on the small bed, it was just right! Soon she was fast asleep.

When the three bears returned,
Papa Bear said, "SOMEONE'S BEEN
SITTING IN MY CHAIR!"

Mama Bear said, "Someone's been
sitting in my chair!"

Baby Bear said, "Someone's been sitting
in my chair, and it's broken to bits!"

Then Papa Bear said, "SOMEONE'S
BEEN EATING MY PORRIDGE!"

Mama Bear said, "Someone's been eating
my porridge!"

Baby Bear said, "Someone's been eating
my porridge, and it's all gone!"

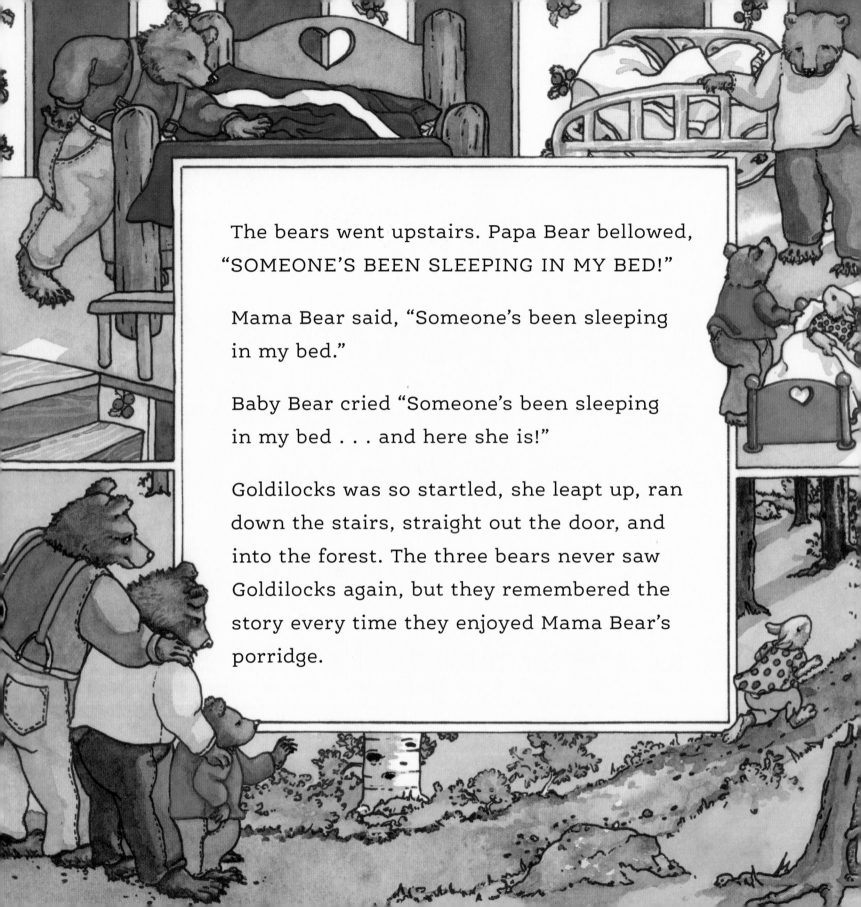

The bears went upstairs. Papa Bear bellowed, "SOMEONE'S BEEN SLEEPING IN MY BED!"

Mama Bear said, "Someone's been sleeping in my bed."

Baby Bear cried "Someone's been sleeping in my bed . . . and here she is!"

Goldilocks was so startled, she leapt up, ran down the stairs, straight out the door, and into the forest. The three bears never saw Goldilocks again, but they remembered the story every time they enjoyed Mama Bear's porridge.

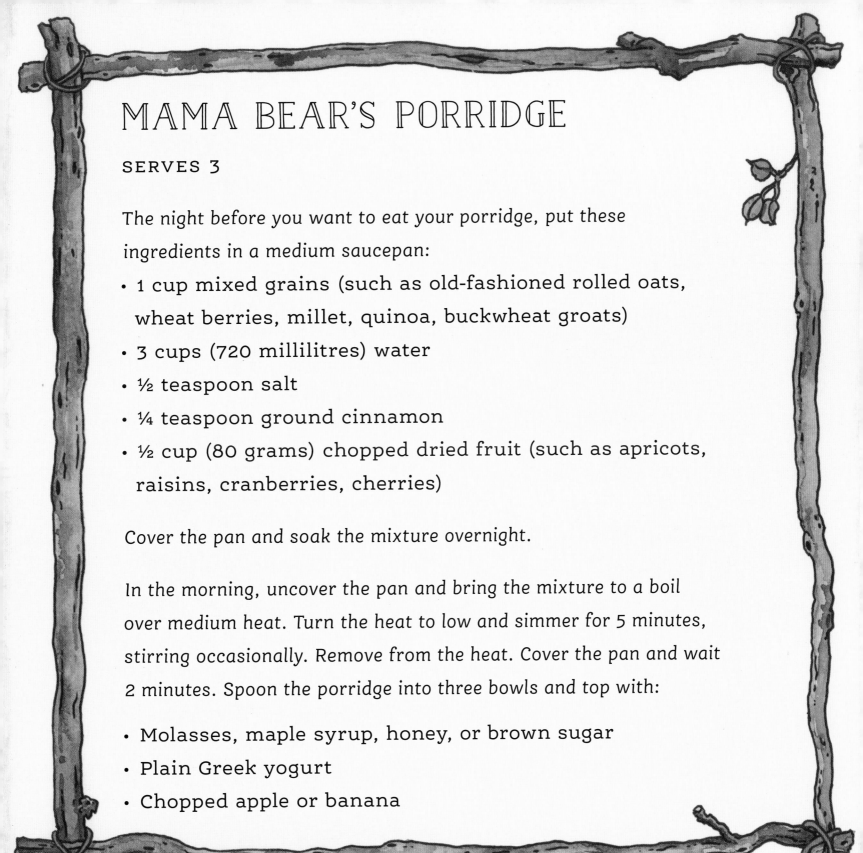

MAMA BEAR'S PORRIDGE

SERVES 3

The night before you want to eat your porridge, put these ingredients in a medium saucepan:

- 1 cup mixed grains (such as old-fashioned rolled oats, wheat berries, millet, quinoa, buckwheat groats)
- 3 cups (720 millilitres) water
- ½ teaspoon salt
- ¼ teaspoon ground cinnamon
- ½ cup (80 grams) chopped dried fruit (such as apricots, raisins, cranberries, cherries)

Cover the pan and soak the mixture overnight.

In the morning, uncover the pan and bring the mixture to a boil over medium heat. Turn the heat to low and simmer for 5 minutes, stirring occasionally. Remove from the heat. Cover the pan and wait 2 minutes. Spoon the porridge into three bowls and top with:

- Molasses, maple syrup, honey, or brown sugar
- Plain Greek yogurt
- Chopped apple or banana

THE END

Pease porridge hot,
Pease porridge cold,
Pease porridge in the pot,
Nine days old.

Star light, star bright,
First star I see tonight,
I wish I may, I wish I might,
Have the wish I wish tonight.

Golden slumbers kiss your eyes,
Smiles awake you when you rise.
Sleep pretty baby, do not cry,
And I will sing a lullaby.

GOOD NIGHT.